Coral
the Reef
Fairy

by Daisy Meadows

SCHOLASTIC INC.

The Earth Fairies must be dreaming
If they think they can escape my scheming.
My goblins are by far the greenest,
And I am definitely the meanest.

Seven fairies out to save the earth?
This very idea fills me with mirth!
I'm sure the world has had enough
Of fairy magic and all that stuff.

So I'm going to steal the fairies' wands
And send them into human lands.
The fairies will think all is lost,
Defeated again—by me, Jack Frost!

Contents

Magic Sparkles

Kirsty Tate grinned as she stepped onto the beach. "This looks *fun*!" she exclaimed, gazing around in excitement.

Her best friend, Rachel Walker, was close behind. "And there's so much to do," she said, her eyes bright. "Where should we go first?"

The two girls had come with their parents to Rainspell Beach, where the local surfing club was holding a "Save the Coral Reefs" event. As Kirsty and Rachel looked around, they could see a crowd of people dancing to the lively beat of a samba band, a line of food stands that all smelled delicious, and an information center surrounded by flags displaying pictures of bright, colorful tropical fish.

"Maybe we should split up and meet back here in an hour for lunch?" Mr. Walker, Rachel's dad, suggested.

"Good idea," Rachel replied. "How about we meet you at the information center at twelve?" She slipped an arm through Kirsty's. "Come on, let's explore." The girls made their way into the crowd, enjoying the hustle and bustle of the event. They were on Rainspell

Island for a school break. So far, they'd
had a very exciting few days helping
their new fairy friends, the Earth Fairies.

"There's another good reason for going
off on our own," Kirsty said, thinking
about the
adventures
they'd had
lately. "We
might meet
another fairy
today."

Rachel grinned
and crossed her fingers. "Here's hoping!"
she said.

At the start of the week, Kirsty and
Rachel had magically transported
themselves to Fairyland to ask King
Oberon and Queen Titania for their help

in cleaning up the human world. The girls had met seven fairies-in-training who each had a special mission. When their training was complete, they would become the Earth Fairies. Their jobs would be to help save the environment in both the human world and in Fairyland. But before the fairies had received their wands and could start work, Jack Frost had appeared. He'd declared his goblins were the only truly "green" creatures and had ordered them to steal the magic wands and hide them in the human world!

Now Kirsty noticed that Rachel was looking around expectantly. Kirsty guessed she was hoping a fairy would instantly appear.

Kirsty gave her a nudge, and said in a low voice, "Remember what Queen Titania always says — there's no point looking for magic."

Rachel nodded. "I know — it'll find us," she agreed. "OK, let's go and learn about coral reefs."

The two friends wandered over to an information booth that had lots of colorful pictures pinned up.

As they got closer, they could see that the pictures were of a tropical reef, with rainbow-colored fish swimming around twisty coral. "Doesn't the coral look amazing?" Kirsty said, pointing at it. "The shapes make them look like weird plants."

"Well, coral *is* alive," said a curly-haired woman behind the booth. "Did you know that coral is a living, breathing organism?"

"It is?" Rachel asked in surprise. "I thought it was just rock."

The woman shook her head. "No," she

said. "It's alive—although more and more coral is becoming damaged and dying these days."

"How does it become damaged?" Kirsty asked. She remembered all the pretty pink-and-white coral she and Rachel had seen when they'd helped Shannon the Ocean Fairy find her enchanted pearls.

"Climate change is a big problem," the curly-haired woman replied. "Coral reefs need to live in a certain temperature range. But the oceans have become warmer, which means the coral gets sick and dies. Other things can damage the coral, too, like when people or boats disturb it. Sometimes just touching coral is enough to kill it."

Rachel and Kirsty both felt sad. While they'd been helping the Earth Fairies, they'd learned  a lot about things like climate change. They knew how much harm was being done to the planet.

They thanked the woman and wandered farther down the beach, past the samba band and some of the food booths. It was a sunny day and unseasonably warm. "I love the way the sea sparkles in the light," Kirsty said, looking out at the waves that rushed in, leaving foam on the sand.

"Something over there is sparkling, too," Rachel said, pointing to the far end of the beach. "Look!"

The girls stared at a rock pool near the beach's edge, where the cliffs reached the waves.

Rachel was right—something in the pool appeared to be glimmering. The incredibly bright light danced around the surrounding rocks.

The two girls felt curious as they walked toward it. Then, as they drew closer to the rocks, Rachel let out a gasp of delight. Climbing out of the tide pool was a shiny pink crab . . . and on its back, dangling a foot in the water and leaving a trail of sparkly bubbles, was a tiny, smiling fairy!

Into the Sea

"It's Coral the Reef Fairy!" Kirsty said with excitement.

"Hello again," Coral called, waving at them. Her shoulder-length blond hair was cut in a sporty bob. She wore a bright pink-and-orange top, a ruffled yellow-and-orange skirt, and a pretty pink necklace with a coral design dangling from it.

Rachel and Kirsty smiled as Coral thanked the crab and fluttered toward them. "There's been a sighting of my wand," she told Kirsty and Rachel. "I was hoping you'd come with me to try and get it back?"

"Of course," Rachel said at once. "Where was it spotted?"

"Near one of the biggest reefs," Coral replied. "A crab saw three goblins over there. One of them has my wand. Apparently, they're not doing a very good job of hiding it."

Kirsty and Rachel exchanged glances.

That didn't surprise them! Jack Frost's goblins might be sneaky, but they weren't exactly the most clever creatures in Fairyland.

"We've got a long way to go, but I have a little bit of magic, so I should be able to take us all there," Coral said.

Rachel glanced around quickly, making sure nobody was watching. Luckily, the three of them were at the far end of the beach, tucked away from everyone. They were virtually out of sight.

Coral saw Rachel looking around. "I can work my magic so it will seem as if no time has passed while you're with me," she assured the girls. "Nobody will notice that you're gone."

"Great," said Kirsty, feeling excited. "Let's go!"

Coral smiled and waved her hand. A cloud of pink-and-white fairy dust fell over Kirsty and Rachel, and they immediately began to shrink, until they were the same size as Coral,

with pretty wings on their backs!

"OK," said Coral, "now we need to get you into the water. . . ."

Kirsty bit her lip as Coral waved her hand again. Into the water? Even though the sun was shining, she was quite sure the sea would be freezing! She gazed down at the water doubtfully . . . but then saw that two bubbles had  appeared on the surface. They were both glistening with golden sparkles.

"Take one of these and put it over your head," Coral said. "It'll help you breathe underwater."

"Oh, we did this when we met Shannon," Rachel said. "Kirsty, do you remember?"

She took one of the bubbles and pulled it over her head. It looked like an old-fashioned diving helmet. Then, with a pop, the bubble disappeared.

Kirsty did the same, and then the three friends fluttered into the ocean. To Kirsty's surprise, the water felt fairly warm as they ducked under the waves. "Thank goodness!" She laughed. "I thought it was going to be really cold— but it feels great in here."

Coral grinned at the look of relief on

her face. "My fairy magic will keep us all warm and dry," she said. "Are you ready? Then off we go!"

She took Kirsty and Rachel's hands, then softly spoke some magical-sounding words. A second later, the three friends were jetting at top speed through the water.

They were going so fast, Kirsty could hardly see. She could only make out blurred colors and streams of bubbles as the magic carried them through the rushing water. It was like the fastest amusement-park ride she'd ever been on. *"Wheeeeee!"* she cried in excitement. "This is amazing!"

A Funny Fish

After a few moments, Kirsty and Rachel felt themselves slowing down. The underwater world swung into focus as they came to a stop, and they could see once more. Both girls gazed around.

The water surrounding them was a clear aquamarine-blue, and schools of brightly colored fish swam in all directions. "Isn't it beautiful?" Kirsty exclaimed.

"And there's the coral reef!" Rachel said, pointing in front of her. The reef stretched a long way into the distance, and they all gazed at its bony structure. It looked like a million fingers reaching up. Colorful anemones grew in the crevices, their skinny fronds waving with the current. All kinds of fish and other sea creatures swam

through and

around

the reef.

The sand

below

sparkled

gold, and

large white

shells lay on the seabed.

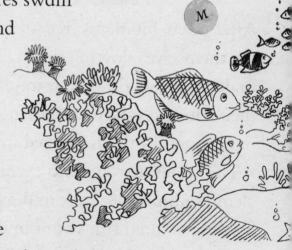

"It's like another world down here," Kirsty marveled, taking it in. Then her mouth fell open in surprise. "Look at that fish!" she cried, pointing. "Is it really *juggling*?"

They all looked at the orange-and-white striped fish. It was skillfully throwing and catching tiny white shells with its fins. Coral grinned. "It's a clown fish," she said.

"Let's go and say hello. He might have seen the goblins."

The three friends swam over to the clown fish.

"Hello, hello, hello," he said, still juggling. "What's the fastest creature underwater?"

"Hi," Coral said. "I have no idea. What *is* the fastest creature underwater?"

"A motor-pike!" The clown fish chuckled, dropping his shells with laughter. "Get it? A motor-*pike*!"

Kirsty and Rachel giggled. They knew a pike was

a kind of fish. "Excuse me," Rachel said
politely. "We were wondering if—?"

"Knock, knock," the clown fish
interrupted.

"Who's there?" Kirsty, Rachel, and
Coral asked in chorus.

"Whelk," said the clown fish.

"Whelk who?"

"Welcome to
the reef. Pleased
to meet you!"
The clown
fish hooted,
slapping his
sides with his
fins. "Get it?
Whelk-ome!"

"We get it." Kirsty
smiled. "I don't suppose you've seen—?"

"What did the lobster say to the clam?" the clown fish interrupted, tossing one of the white shells up again and balancing it on his nose.

"Listen, we really need your help," Coral insisted. "We're looking for—"

"Stop being so shellfish!" the clown fish shouted, spinning a somersault as he laughed at his own joke.

"Please!" Rachel cried. "Can you be serious for one minute?"

The clown fish stopped laughing and stared at them, as if seeing them for the first time.

"Serious?" he repeated. "It's not my job to be serious," he told them. Then he thought for a moment. "Of course," he went on, "if I *was* going to be serious, I might tell you that I'd seen some strange green creatures swimming near the reef earlier. They were climbing all over it, not realizing that they might be hurting the coral. Not realizing that at all."

"Thank you," Rachel said, relieved to have gotten a straight answer at last. "That's really helpful. Where were they?"

The clown fish pointed a fin. "That way," he said. Then he smiled. "I say, I say, I say . . ." he began.

But Coral motioned Kirsty and Rachel away. "Sorry, we've got to go," she called to the clown fish as they swam off in the direction he'd shown them. "Thanks again! Great jokes!"

The three friends swam into the reef. Kirsty and Rachel both gazed at the sights around them. There were fish of every shape and color, unusual sea plants sprouting from the sand, crabs scuttling, and majestic sea turtles who raised their flippers in greeting. Then came a shout. "You're It!"

Coral's eyes grew wide. "Goblins," she whispered. "It sounds like they're very nearby!"

Dangerous Water

Coral grabbed Kirsty and Rachel and pulled them behind a large clump of seaweed. She peeked through its fronds, then put her finger to her lips as she turned back to the goblins. "The goblins are right in front of us," she whispered. "You should see the way they're jumping all over the reef. They could cause terrible damage doing that!"

Kirsty and Rachel peeked out at the three goblins. They were all wearing helmets and flippers, and seemed to be playing tag around the reef, leaping from one part to another without a care. Rachel nudged her friends as she saw what one of the goblins was holding.

"The wand!" She gasped. "Right there!"

"The sooner I get it back, the better,"
Coral fumed. "What is he *doing* with it?"

The three friends stared in horror as
they saw the goblin poking holes in the
reef as he tried
to tag another
goblin
with the
wand.
"Ow!"
squealed
a small
yellow
fish as
the goblin accidentally jabbed it.

"I can't bear to watch anymore," Coral
said. "Come on, let's try and get the
wand from him."

Coral, Kirsty, and Rachel swam out from their hiding place toward the goblins . . . but before they'd gone very far, one of the goblins shouted a warning cry. "Over there! A horrible fairy and her friends! Quick, let's swim!"

The goblins immediately swam through the water away from Coral, Kirsty, and Rachel.

"Hurry," Coral shouted to Kirsty and Rachel. "They're getting away. After them!"

The three friends sped after the goblins,
keeping a close eye on the one carrying
the wand—they could not
let him out of their sight!
But it was difficult
to swim quickly
through the reef.
Its twisty structure
meant that Kirsty,
Rachel, and Coral
had to be careful
and avoid touching
it. They had
to slow down.
Unfortunately, the
goblins did not care. They
carelessly bashed into the reef with their
big flippers. It wasn't long before the
speedy goblins had pulled so far ahead

that Rachel, Kirsty,
and Coral had
completely
lost sight
of them.

"We don't
even know
which
direction
they went."
Kirsty
sighed.
"They could be
anywhere by now!"

Rachel was about to speak when a
huge shadow loomed over the three of
them, blocking the sunlight and making
the water feel colder and much darker.

She looked up anxiously, wondering if a shark, or another large sea creature above, was causing the shadow. But it was neither. "It's a boat," she realized, staring up at its underside.

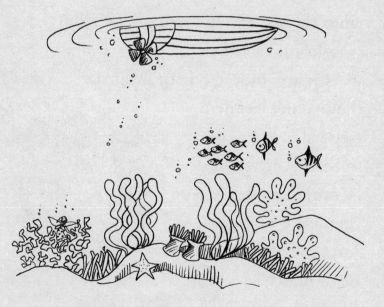

"Yes," agreed Coral in dismay. "And look what just jumped off it!" She pointed at the water, which was churning with splashes and bubbles. As the bubbles cleared, Kirsty and Rachel saw a group of people who had dived into the sea. They were all wearing masks and snorkels.

"Quick, hide!" Kirsty gasped. "We can't let them see us!"

She, Rachel, and Coral darted behind a boulder and peered around it to watch the swimmers. Some carried special

underwater cameras and photographed
the sea creatures, making excited
gestures to one another. Some wore big
flippers—and
Coral groaned
as she noticed
several people
clumsily kicking
the reef with
them.

"Oh, no—
more damage,"
she said sadly. "I'm sure they're not doing
it on purpose, but they're not being
careful enough. Let's see if I can help."
She waved her hand in a pattern
and muttered some magic words.
A stream of pink bubbles appeared near
the snorkelers and surrounded their

flippers. The bubbles gently moved the people away from the coral reef.

"That's better," Rachel said. "Nice work, Coral! Now, let's keep looking for the goblins. We've got to find them before any of the snorkelers spot them."

Kirsty nodded at once. She knew that it would be a disaster if any other humans found out about Fairyland or its magical inhabitants. "Well, there's no sign of them here," she said, looking around, "so maybe—"

She stopped talking when she spotted something even more alarming than goblins. 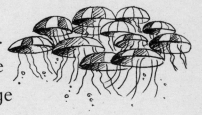 Floating on the surface of the water was a large school of jellyfish. Their pale pink bodies gleamed, and a mass of ribbony tentacles dangled in their wake.

"Get back!" Coral warned, grabbing Kirsty and Rachel and pulling them away as the jellyfish drifted dangerously close. "If any of us are stung, we'll be in big trouble!"

Bubble
Trouble

Kirsty, Rachel, and Coral swam quickly
down to the seafloor to avoid the
jellyfish. A shout went out from one of
the snorkelers, who'd also spotted the
jellyfish. The group of people went back
to their boat, looking nervous.

After a minute or two, the jellyfish had
passed by, and the three friends were
able to set off in search of the goblins

again. They plunged deeper into the reef,
looking everywhere for a glimpse of
green. Rachel had lost count of how
many times she'd mistaken a patch of
jade seaweed for a
goblin leg. Then,
all of a sudden,
she heard voices
again.

"He shoots . . .
and he scores!
What a goal!"
Kirsty and
Coral had
heard the voices,
too, and they all
stopped swimming
to hide behind the reef and
peek out.

The goblins were a short distance away. This time they were kicking and throwing a ball of seaweed through the water. "And look—they're using the reef as a goal!" Kirsty sighed. Coral had had enough. She swam out, furious. "You goblins are damaging the reef," she told them. "You have to be more careful—it's a living thing, you know!"

The three goblins
stuck out their
tongues as if they
didn't care.

"We're just
having a little
fun," the first
one told Coral
scornfully.

"Why don't
you keep your
fairy nose out
of our business?" the second goblin
chimed in.

"Just ignore her," said the third
goblin, who was carrying the wand.
"She can't do anything to move us
away from the reef while I've got
this—and she knows it!"

Coral gritted her teeth and seemed on the verge of losing her temper, but Rachel whispered in her ear. "Actually, you *can* move them if you want to," she reminded Coral in a low voice. "The same way you moved the snorkelers away from the reef."

Kirsty, who'd come close enough to hear, joined in. "And maybe you can use your magic to move other things, too—like your wand, out of the goblin's hand!" she suggested.

"I'll try," said Coral, "but my magic might not be strong enough."

She took a deep breath, then waved her hands and chanted some magic words. A stream of pink bubbles suddenly appeared around the wand, and the goblin who was holding it looked startled.

"Hey!" he yelled, as the bubbles dragged him forward a little. "Something's pulling this wand. Help me!"

His two friends swam to him at once
and grabbed ahold of him, tugging him
back. "Hold on tight," one of them urged
him.

"Don't worry," the goblin with the
wand replied. "I'm not letting go of
it—not ever!"

He clung on and after a few minutes,
the bubbles popped. He yelled at Coral.
"Is that the best you can do? Pathetic!"
Then he kicked the seaweed ball back to
the other goblins. "Let's go back to our
game."

Kirsty's shoulders slumped in disappointment. It hadn't worked. "We need another plan," she said. "And quick, before they decide to swim away again."

Rachel gazed around, hoping to find inspiration. She shivered when she saw that another cluster of jellyfish had appeared above them . . . and then an idea popped into her head.

"I think I've got it," she said slowly, thinking it through. "What if the goblin thought the wand was leading him into danger? Surely *that* would be enough to make him let go of it?"

Good-bye, Goblins!

A frown creased Coral's face. "What do you mean?" she asked.

"I mean, what if you could make the wand move again, but this time don't send it toward us," Rachel said, the words tumbling out of her with eagerness. "Send it toward the jellyfish. If the goblin thought the wand was dragging him up to the stinging jellyfish, I bet he would let go of it!"

Coral's eyes twinkled. "Good thinking, Rachel!" she said.

Kirsty grinned at her friend's clever plan and then spoke in a voice loud enough for the goblins to hear. "Come on, let's leave the goblins to play their game. It's too dangerous to hang around here anymore."

The goblin with the wand looked triumphant. "At last—someone is making sense," he sneered. "Hear that? Dangerous, she said. She's obviously scared silly of us goblins. And she should be!"

Coral stared up at the jellyfish, pretending to be terrified. "Yes, those are the really dangerous jellyfish," she said loudly to Kirsty and Rachel. "Come on, girls, we have to get away quickly."

The goblins all looked up. Their faces dropped as soon as they spotted the jellyfish. "Oh, no," one of them said fearfully. "They're not scared of us. They're scared of those jellyfish!"

Kirsty, Rachel, and Coral turned and

swam away from the goblins, then hid
behind the reef so they could keep an eye
on them.

All the goblins looked worried about
the jellyfish, but it
seemed like none
of them wanted
to admit it. "I'm
not scared,"
blustered one.
"The jellyfish
are right up
near the
surface and
we're all the
way down
here. We'll be
fine, I'm sure."
Coral winked

at Kirsty and Rachel. "Let's see if he's still so sure after I do this," she whispered, waving her hands and muttering some magic words.

A stream of bubbles immediately moved through the water and surrounded the wand, tugging it upward. The goblin holding the wand was taken by surprise as it dragged him toward the jellyfish.

"Hey! What's happening?" he yelped, his eyes bulging with fear as he rushed through the water. "Help me! Help!"

His friends grabbed his legs as he whooshed upward, but this time they couldn't pull him back down. Now all three goblins were heading straight for the cluster of jellyfish.

"*Noooooo!*" they screamed.

"They're going to get us!" wailed the goblin with the wand.

"Let go of the wand, then!" one of his friends shouted.

Rachel and Kirsty could tell by the first goblin's face that he really didn't want to let go, but as he came just inches away from the jellyfish tentacles, he gave a squawk of fright and threw it away. As he let go of the wand, he fell back through the water, and so did his two friends.

Down tumbled the goblins, their arms flailing. Coral zoomed out from her hiding place and used her special bubble magic to bring the wand back into her hand. "Hooray!" she cheered in delight.

"Aarrrrgh!" the goblins shouted as, one by one, they plunged into a huge bed of slimy brown seaweed.

Kirsty and Rachel couldn't help
laughing as the goblins,
all tangled up,
with seaweed
draped over
their heads
and bodies,
broke into
furious
fighting.

"I think
the three
of you should
go back to Fairyland as soon as
possible." Coral chuckled. She waved her
wand to send them on their way with
one last blast of bubble magic. The
bubbles carried the arguing goblins into
the distance, and they vanished.

"That was so funny." Kirsty giggled, and then hugged Coral.

"And it's wonderful that you got your wand back!" Coral smiled. "I know," she said. "I've got a lot of work to do now, to make sure the reefs aren't damaged any further. I feel really flattered that the king and queen have trusted me with such an important job. I'm determined to do my best for them—and for the oceans!" She twirled her wand in her hand. "Thank you for helping me, girls. I should send you back to Rainspell Island now."

Rachel hugged the fairy good-bye. "Glad we could help you," she said. "Bye, Coral."

"Bye!" called Kirsty, just as Coral waved her wand. A stream of sparkling bubbles enveloped the girls and they found themselves whirling around very quickly.

A few moments later, they were back on the beach where they'd started their adventure. They were their usual sizes again, and  completely dry. And, just like Coral had promised, it was as if no time had passed.

"Wow," Rachel said, smiling happily at Kirsty. "That was so exciting."

"Wasn't it amazing, being near a real coral reef?" Kirsty sighed. "I hope Coral can keep it healthy with her magic."

Rachel nodded. "We'll have to help her," she said. "We can spread the word about the problems facing the reefs so that everyone knows how to protect them."

"Maybe we can make some posters to put up in the surf store and the snorkel rental shop?" Kirsty suggested. "We should especially mention being careful with flippers around the reef. That will get the message out, won't it?"

"Good idea," Rachel said.

Kirsty linked an arm through Rachel's as they wandered back to the food stands. "This is turning out to be such an amazing week," she said. "I can't wait to see what will happen tomorrow!"

Coral the Reef Fairy now has her wand back!
Next, Rachel and Kirsty need to help . . .

Lily
the Rain Forest Fairy!

Join their next adventure
in this special sneak peek. . . .

Food From the Forest

"Look, Kirsty," Rachel Walker called as she hurried through the trees, "I think I found some wild onions!"

"Oh, great!" Kirsty Tate, Rachel's best friend, ran to join her, swinging her basket. The two girls were on a nature walk in the forest near their vacation cottages on Rainspell Island, where they were spending the school break with their families.

Rachel and Kirsty knelt down and gazed at the onion plants. They had long, thin leaves and greenish-white flowers. The girls knew that, not so far underground, were the onion bulbs.

"The Junior Naturalist class we went to this morning was fun, wasn't it, Kirsty?" Rachel said with a smile. "I never realized there were so many things growing wild on Rainspell Island that you can eat. Do you have the soup recipe the teacher gave us?"

Kirsty took a leaflet labeled MUSHROOM SOUP out of her basket.

"Remember, Jo told us that we should only take as much as we need," Kirsty reminded Rachel. "Otherwise the plant won't be able to reseed itself, and then there won't be new onion plants next year."

Rachel checked the recipe ingredients. Then she carefully pulled some of the onion bulbs and put them in Kirsty's basket. The girls had already collected some sprigs of sweet-smelling wild thyme and other herbs.

"Now we just have to find some mushrooms, and we can make soup for dinner tonight!" Rachel jumped to her feet. "We have to remember to check the booklet about mushrooms that Jo gave us, because we need to make sure the ones we find aren't poisonous."

"Isn't it amazing how many different plants and animals there are in the forest?" Kirsty remarked as they wandered along the path again.

RAINBOW magic™

Which Magical Fairies Have You Met?

- ☐ The Rainbow Fairies
- ☐ The Weather Fairies
- ☐ The Jewel Fairies
- ☐ The Pet Fairies
- ☐ The Dance Fairies
- ☐ The Music Fairies
- ☐ The Sports Fairies
- ☐ The Party Fairies
- ☐ The Ocean Fairies
- ☐ The Night Fairies
- ☐ The Magical Animal Fairies
- ☐ The Princess Fairies
- ☐ The Superstar Fairies
- ☐ The Fashion Fairies
- ☐ The Sugar & Spice Fairies

SCHOLASTIC

Find all of your favorite fairy friends at
scholastic.com/rainbowmagic

HIT entertainment

RMFAIRY

RAINBOW magic™

Which Magical Fairies Have You Met?

3 stories in each one!

- ☐ Joy the Summer Vacation Fairy
- ☐ Holly the Christmas Fairy
- ☐ Kylie the Carnival Fairy
- ☐ Stella the Star Fairy
- ☐ Shannon the Ocean Fairy
- ☐ Trixie the Halloween Fairy
- ☐ Gabriella the Snow Kingdom Fairy
- ☐ Juliet the Valentine Fairy
- ☐ Mia the Bridesmaid Fairy
- ☐ Flora the Dress-Up Fairy
- ☐ Paige the Christmas Play Fairy
- ☐ Emma the Easter Fairy
- ☐ Cara the Camp Fairy
- ☐ Destiny the Rock Star Fairy
- ☐ Belle the Birthday Fairy
- ☐ Olympia the Games Fairy
- ☐ Selena the Sleepover Fairy
- ☐ Cheryl the Christmas Tree Fairy
- ☐ Florence the Friendship Fairy
- ☐ Lindsay the Luck Fairy
- ☐ Brianna the Tooth Fairy
- ☐ Autumn the Falling Leaves Fairy
- ☐ Keira the Movie Star Fairy
- ☐ Addison the April Fool's Day Fairy

■ SCHOLASTIC

Find all of your favorite fairy friends at
scholastic.com/rainbowmagic

HIT entertainment

RMSPECIAL12

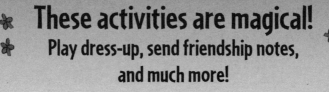

These activities are magical!
Play dress-up, send friendship notes, and much more!

■SCHOLASTIC
www.scholastic.com
www.rainbowmagiconline.com

HiT entertainment

RMACTIV